THE PUPPY PLACE

MOLLY

Don't miss any of these other stories by Ellen Miles!

Bandit

Baxter

Bear

Bella

Buddy

Chewy and Chica

Cocoa

Cody

Flash

Goldie

Honey

Jack

Lucky

Lucy

Maggie and Max

Mocha

Molly

Moose

Muttley

Noodle

Oscar

Patches

Princess

Pugsley

Rascal

Rocky

Scout

Shadow

Snowball

Sweetie

Teddy

Ziggy

MOLLY

ELLEN MILES

SCHOLASTIC INC.

For Jarvis, Benjamin, Sasha, and Jameson

No part of this publication may be reproduced, stored in a retrieval system, or transmitted in any form or by any means, electronic, mechanical, photocopying, recording, or otherwise, without written permission of the publisher. For information regarding permission, write to Scholastic Inc., Attention: Permissions Department, 557 Broadway, New York, NY 10012.

ISBN 978-0-545-46242-6

Cover art by Tim O'Brien
Original cover design by Steve Scott

12 11 10 9 8 7 6 5 4   13 14 15 16 17 18/0

Printed in the U.S.A.   40

First printing, April 2013

CHAPTER ONE

Noisy! Man, was it noisy. How could a few little kids make such a huge amount of noise? Charles almost wanted to put his hands over his ears. Penny's Place, his little brother's day care, was not always so loud. Sometimes when Charles and his mom came to pick up his brother, it was pretty quiet. Kids would be napping, or sitting in a circle listening to Miss Penny read a book, or drawing with crayons at the big art table.

Not today. Today there were three little girls in the dress-up corner, squabbling over a red cape. In another corner, two boys yelled as they banged blocks together. A tiny girl in a purple striped sweater lay on a couch, kicking her legs and crying loudly as one of the teachers tried to comfort her, and a parade of older kids marched through the playroom tootling on horns, crashing cymbals together, and banging on drums and tambourines.

Then Charles heard something else. Even over all that noise, he thought he recognized his own brother's special yell. He cocked his head to hear better. Then he was sure. "That's the Bean," he said. "Where is he?"

"I think Adam is in the kitchen with Miss Penny." The teacher who was helping the little girl barely looked up as she answered.

Adam. That sounded so strange. At home, he was always just the Bean. But Charles thought maybe it was a good idea for his brother to start getting used to his real name before he went to kindergarten. "He doesn't sound happy," Charles said. He ran toward the sound of the Bean's wail, and found him in the kitchen.

The Bean stood below a high counter, fists clenched and face bright red, screaming, "Up! I want to be up!"

On top of the counter sat a boy named Daniel. Charles knew it was Daniel, because he was wearing a Spider-Man shirt. Daniel *always* wore a Spider-Man shirt. In fact, he was known as "Spidey" at Miss Penny's. And not just because of the shirt. According to Miss Penny, Daniel really was just like Spider-Man. He could climb anything. He seemed to see the whole world as a giant jungle gym. If you took your eyes off him for one second, you could be sure that he would scramble up, up, and away.

"Okay, Spidey," Miss Penny was saying calmly, just as Charles walked in. She scooped Daniel up off the counter and set him back down on the floor.

Charles had noticed that Miss Penny was always calm, no matter what. The fish tank could fall over, the muffin batter could explode, the toilet could overflow — anything. Miss Penny, with her happy red cheeks and thick blond braids, would set things right. Not only that, she would do it with a smile on her face and a soft tone in her voice.

Right now, the Bean did not have a soft tone in his voice. He was still yelling his head off, even though his friend was back down on the floor. Charles went over to put his arms around his little brother, hugging him close and lifting him up a little. "It's okay, Beanie," he murmured into his ear. The Bean was usually a happy guy, but when he got upset, nobody could calm him down the way Charles could.

Mom always said Charles was good with little kids. Charles was proud of that. He was good with puppies, too. And not just his own puppy, Buddy. The Petersons — Charles and his older sister, Lizzie, and the Bean and Mom and Dad — were a foster family for puppies. They took care of puppies who needed homes, and helped find a forever family for each one.

Now, hugging the Bean, Charles whispered again into his ear, "Let's go home and see Buddy, okay?"

The Bean had stopped shouting, and now he nodded and smiled. "Buddy," he said. "Buddy-Puddy-Muddy-Wuddy-Doody!"

"That's right," said Charles, ignoring that last word. The Bean liked to say "bad" words sometimes, just to get a reaction out of everyone. "Buddy's waiting for us."

Miss Penny smiled. "You're such a terrific big brother, Charles. I bet you're a huge help to your parents."

Charles shrugged. Behind him, his mom put her hands on his shoulders. "He sure is," she said. "He'll be a help on our field trip next week, too. I've asked Charles to come along when we go to Fable Farm." Mom had signed up to be a field trip helper. So far she'd gone along on the day care's trips to the library, the firehouse, and a bakery. But this time she was in charge. She was planning a special trip for the Penny's Place kids, a visit to a local farm where they had ducks and geese and sheep and all kinds of vegetables and flowers, too. Charles was going to get to leave school early that day just so he could come along.

"Oh, that's terrific," said Miss Penny. "We're going to have a big group that day."

"Charles and the Bean and I will go to the farm in the next few days," Mom told Miss Penny. "We thought it might be a good idea to check things out ahead of time so we can plan our visit."

"Wonderful," said Miss Penny.

Just then, the Bean pulled himself away from Charles's hug and pointed high up in the air. "Up, up, up, up, up," he yelled.

Everyone turned to look. Daniel waved and grinned at them — from on top of the fridge.

"How does he *do* that?" Mom asked. "I never even saw —"

Miss Penny just laughed as she strode over to lift Daniel down. "You can't take your eyes off him for a second," she said to Mom and Charles. To Daniel and the Bean, she said, "Go get your things from your cubbies and help Annabelle straighten up the block corner. It's almost time to go home."

"How do *you* do it?" Mom asked Miss Penny, once Daniel and the Bean had been shooed into the other room. "I mean, there's something happening every minute here, but you always keep your cool. And the kids seem to respond when you tell them to do something. I think the Bean listens to you better than he listens to me."

Miss Penny shrugged. "I'm used to it, I guess," she said. "But there's one thing I'm *not* used to, and I think I need your help." She gestured toward a door at the back of the kitchen. "She's out here."

"She? Who?" Charles followed along, curious.

Miss Penny unlocked the door with a key she pulled out of her pocket. "Her name is Molly," she said, as she pushed open the door to a small pantry.

Charles only had one moment to wonder why Miss Penny would be keeping a little girl in that room. As the door swung open, he realized that Molly was not a little girl.

Molly was a puppy.

CHAPTER TWO

"Wow," Charles said. "What a cutie."

Molly sat at attention, with her ears on alert and her brown eyes shining. Her stubby tail wagged in anticipation. She did not jump up, like some excited puppies did, or shy away, like some timid puppies might have. She just waited, grinning a puppy grin, to see what would happen next.

Molly was a stocky, solid pup, mostly dark chocolate brown with beautiful markings in shades of lighter brown. She had huge chunky feet, a big square head with droopy jowls, and floppy triangular ears. She had light brown oval spots over each eye — Charles had once read that "eyebrow" spots like that were known as "pumpkinseeds" — and they twitched as she looked with interest from one person to another.

Oh, how nice. Company! I was getting a little lonely in here.

Miss Penny went over to pet Molly. "Good girl," she said. "You really are a very good girl." She turned to Charles and his mom and held up her hands. "She's a sweetie. It's just — how can I keep her? I run a day care. My house is full of little kids every day. I have to think about what to feed them, what to teach them, how to keep them safe. How could I possibly handle a dog on top of all that — even if it was okay to have a dog at a day care, which it isn't?"

Charles couldn't believe it. Miss Penny actually

seemed flustered. He had never seen her that way before. "Where did Molly come from?" Charles asked. He went closer to Molly and held out a hand for her to sniff. "Is she okay with kids? How old is she? What are you going to do with her?"

Miss Penny laughed. "So many questions. First of all, she's almost a year old and yes — she seems to be very gentle with kids. Not that I've let her into my day care. I can't have a dog I barely know in with the children I'm taking care of. But she was with my nephew and nieces yesterday and she was fine with them. They were climbing all over her and she didn't bat an eye."

Hearing that, Charles bent down to pet Molly. She leaned into him and let him scratch between her ears, sighing with contentment.

"And as far as where she came from," Miss Penny continued, "that's kind of a sad story. She belonged to my aunt Tabby. Crabby Tabby, as she was known. Tabby was always a huge dog lover, but she was not so fond of people."

"Was?" Mom asked. "Did she —"

Penny nodded. "She passed away last week. Right up to the end, she was living on her own. She wouldn't let anybody help her — except me. I used to come over once or twice a week to bring her groceries, do a little cleaning, take Molly out for a stroll, that sort of thing. Aunt Tabby always said I was a hard worker and a good soul." Miss Penny looked down at the floor. "I guess that's why she left Molly to me, along with enough money to take care of her very nicely for the rest of her doggy life. I just found out yesterday, when I met with my aunt's lawyer — and he had Molly with him. I really had no choice. I had to take the puppy."

They all turned to look at Molly. She gazed back at them with warm, brown eyes.

"So, what now?" Mom asked.

Miss Penny shrugged. "I don't know. Molly is wonderful, and I want to carry out my aunt's wishes — but I just don't see how I can. It's not fair to keep a dog locked up by herself in a tiny room all day long. But I can't let her out into the rest of the house, either. I have a lot of kids in my care, and I doubt their parents would be too happy about having a dog loose in the day care."

Charles noticed that Molly seemed to be listening to every word. Poor puppy. She needed a home. "Mom?" Charles looked up at his mother. "Maybe we can help. Maybe we could foster Molly for a few days, just until Miss Penny figures things out."

"Oh, would you? Could you?" Miss Penny looked relieved. "That would be —"

Bang! A loud sound came from inside the house, followed by a wail. Molly leapt to her feet, her head cocked.

What was that? Is everyone all right?

"Oh, dear," said Miss Penny. "That sounded like Spidey." She disappeared through the door in a flash, leaving Mom and Charles with Molly, who whimpered as she stared intently at the door.

Charles went over to comfort the pup. "It's okay," he told Molly. Since he didn't hear any more wails, he figured Daniel was fine. Sure enough, he soon heard everyone singing "The Good-bye Song," the one they always sang at Miss Penny's at the end of the day. He hugged Molly close, loving the way her warm, solid body felt in his arms.

Mom raised her eyebrows. "Charles," she began. She did not look happy.

"I know, I know," he said. "I should have asked you first. But it's so perfect. Miss Penny needs help. We foster puppies. Can't we take her, just for a little while?"

"Well . . ." Mom frowned slightly as she studied Molly. "We'd have to check with your dad —"

"Call him!" Charles jumped up.

". . . but I don't see why not," Mom continued, with a smile. "If Miss Penny really would like us to help with Molly."

"Yeah!" Charles threw a fist into the air and then dropped back to his knees to hug Molly while Mom pulled out her phone to call Dad. Maybe the Petersons were about to have a new foster puppy. Lizzie sure would be surprised.

"She seems pretty easygoing and calm," Mom reported into the phone a moment later. "Yes, I think she'd get along with Buddy." She listened for a moment. "All right, then," she said. "We'll be home soon."

"Did you hear that?" Charles whispered into Molly's ear. "It looks like you're coming home with us."

CHAPTER THREE

"And she's really, really cute, and so totally sweet. You should see how gentle she is with the Bean." The next day at school, Charles was using up most of the Sharing Circle time at his class's morning meeting. He had told about how he and his mom had met Molly, and how Miss Penny had agreed that it was probably best for them to take her home that very night. He couldn't stop talking about Molly. Mr. Mason, his teacher, didn't seem to mind. Everyone always liked to hear about the puppies the Petersons fostered.

Bethany threw up her hand. "What kind of dog is Molly?" she asked.

"It's funny. I wasn't sure, but my sister knew the minute we walked into the house. She's a Rottweiler," Charles reported.

Lizzie could always tell what breed dogs were. When you walked down the street with her, she'd name every dog she saw. "Lab, corgi, Greater Swiss Mountain Dog, Weimaraner . . ." Charles had no idea what some of those dogs looked like, but Lizzie did.

Nicky gasped. "Wait. A Rottweiler? In your house? Are you kidding me? They are the meanest, toughest, scariest dogs in the world."

Charles stared at him. "What are you talking about?" he asked. That didn't sound like Molly.

"Everybody knows that," said Nicky. "Rottweilers are really big, and they have huge teeth and strong jaws like a crocodile and they're unpredictable. One minute they're your friend, and the next minute all they want to do is bite you and attack you."

Charles turned to Mr. Mason. "That can't be true," he said. He didn't know much about Rottweilers, but he already knew Molly, and he could not believe that Molly would ever attack anyone. "Lizzie said that Rottweilers are smart and loyal and calm."

Mr. Mason raised his eyebrows. "It sounds like we all need to learn a little more about these dogs." He had a certain smile on his face, an all-too-familiar smile.

Charles groaned inwardly. He could guess what his teacher would say next.

"Charles and Nicky, I'd like you to work together on a report to share with the rest of the class. I'll help you get started on some research, and hopefully we can find out the truth about Rottweilers."

Charles and Nicky looked at each other and rolled their eyes. They should have seen it coming. Mr. Mason used any excuse to assign a report.

Benjamin waved his hand. "It's like with pit bulls," he said. "Everybody says they're really nasty and vicious, but that's not actually always true. My uncle Jarvis has one and she's just a big pussycat. Her name is Sasha. My uncle says that pit bulls get a bad reputation because some people do train them to be mean."

Mr. Mason nodded. "I had a friend in college who had a pit bull. Same thing. He was a nice dog, but everyone was scared of him. I guess sometimes we judge dogs — and people — unfairly." He put his hands on his knees and stood up. "Let's all take a nice stretch and then get out our math workbooks. It's time to start our day."

After math they worked on their science unit, then they had reading buddies, then a special art class where they made posters for the school's spring fair. There was no extra time to start any reports about Rottweilers, which was fine with Charles. It upset him even to think that people would be afraid of a sweet, gentle dog like Molly.

Charles's aunt Amanda came over to meet Molly that afternoon, and Charles told her what Nicky had said. Aunt Amanda knew even more about dogs than Lizzie did. She even ran a doggy day care, where she took care of people's dogs when they were at work or on vacation. Come to think of it, Bowser's Backyard was a lot like Penny's Place — only with dogs instead of kids. There was a kitchen where Aunt Amanda made treats, an indoor and an outdoor play area, and a room for naptime. Sometimes the dogs even did crafts, like paw-painting instead of finger-painting.

"Well, some people do use rotties as guard dogs," said Aunt Amanda. "They are very protective — that's just part of being loyal. If someone tries to hurt their owner, they will do anything to protect the one they love." She rubbed Molly's ears. "And they do grow up to be large pooches, and they do have big teeth and strong jaws. Don't you, sweetie?" she cooed at the puppy. Molly snuggled under Aunt Amanda's hand and looked up at her with her velvety brown eyes.

Me? I'm just a baby.

Charles still could not imagine that this adorable pup would grow up to be mean and scary. "But Molly won't be like that, will she?" he asked.

Aunt Amanda shook her head. "Not if she grows

up with the right kind of owner, the kind who will guide her with a firm hand and teach her to use her strength gently. I truly believe that there are no bad dogs, only bad owners. It doesn't matter what breed a dog is. Any dog can be taught to be vicious — or raised to be loving."

Charles nodded. Maybe he could put that in his report on Rottweilers.

That night after dinner, Charles sat on the living room floor, playing with Buddy and Molly. He noticed that, unlike many of the puppies his family had fostered, Molly never tried to bite his hands or feet. By now, Charles was used to sharp little puppy teeth. He knew that lots of puppies liked to "mouth" people and other dogs. He'd even learned, when he was taking care of a very mouthy Chihuahua named Chewy, that it was good to say "Ouch!" when they did. That helped puppies learn that it was not okay to bite.

But Molly didn't seem to need that lesson. She was naturally gentle. She liked to wrestle with Buddy and let him chase her around the room, but Charles never heard her growl or snarl, even in play.

Until she met Mr. Duck.

When Charles showed her Buddy's well-worn stuffed toy, she leapt at it and grabbed it in her strong jaws. Then she shook it and shook it, making deep, rumbling, growly sounds way down in her throat. Her sharp white teeth flashed as she bit at Mr. Duck's yellow fur, again and again.

When Charles saw those teeth digging into the stuffed toy, his stomach flipped over. He thought of what Nicky had said about Rottweilers being unpredictable. Could it be that Nicky was right? What if Molly turned out to be mean, after all? What if she suddenly decided to bite Charles the way she was biting Mr. Duck?

That night, for the first time ever, Charles did not argue when Lizzie wanted their new foster puppy to sleep in her room. For the first time ever, Charles began to understand what it felt like to be afraid of a dog.

CHAPTER FOUR

Charles had always felt sorry for people who were afraid of dogs. He knew it was just because they didn't understand that most dogs were friendly, and that as long as you approached them gently, checked with their owners, and didn't frighten them, most dogs would never hurt you.

Most dogs.

Now Charles was beginning to wonder. Was Molly like most dogs? Or was she more like the Rottweilers that Nicky had told about, the ones who were nasty and mean?

Aunt Amanda had said that it wasn't about the breed, it was about the owner. And in the middle of the night, when Charles lay worrying about Molly, he suddenly remembered what Miss Penny had told them about Molly's first owner. "Crabby Tabby," they called her. She didn't get along with people. For all Charles knew, Crabby Tabby had trained her dog to be as mean as she was. His eyes popped wide open when he thought of that, and he lay awake for a long time. Was Lizzie safe with Molly in her room? What would he do if he heard growling from down the hall? It would be all his fault if the puppy hurt his sister.

Charles yawned through morning meeting at school the next day, and just shook his head when Mr. Mason asked for an update on Molly. On the playground at recess, he put his hands over his ears when Nicky started talking about pit bulls that were trained to fight each other. And in the afternoon, when he was doing some Internet research for his Rottweiler report, Charles clicked quickly past pictures of Rottweilers wearing spiked collars, or Rottweilers with their huge jaws open in ferocious barking. He tried to focus instead on the positive things he read about Rottweilers — for example, that they were often very good with children.

But later that day, when he and Lizzie walked into the house after school, Molly charged toward them, swinging her head in a strange way and pulling back her lips to show glints of shiny, sharp white teeth. Charles ducked behind Lizzie, terrified. He could have sworn that Molly had grown bigger in the few hours they'd been away. Her beefy chest and strong legs gave her the look of a little tank. And that little tank was rolling straight toward him.

"Oh, Molly." Lizzie dropped to her knees to throw her arms around the puppy. "You're glad to see us, aren't you? Look at your funny smile."

She rubbed Molly's head and patted her sides, and Molly's stubby tail wagged double-time.

I'm so happy you're home! I've been lonely all day. It's so much more fun to be around lots of people.

Lizzie turned to look at Charles. "What's the matter?" she asked.

"Nothing." He shrugged, and stayed put exactly where he was, behind his big sister.

"You're not —" Lizzie turned to stare at him. "Are you afraid of this puppy?"

Charles laughed. It came out sounding fake, like "Ha, ha, ha," but he couldn't help it. "Of course not," he said. Then he thought it might be a good idea to change the subject. "I'm hungry. Wonder what Mom left out for snacks." Quickly, he stepped around Lizzie and Molly, heading for the kitchen.

Charles managed to avoid Molly for the rest of the afternoon, without making it look too obvious. He took his snack of apple slices and string cheese up to his room, claiming that he had to work on his report. He let Buddy follow him, but he closed the door once his own sweet, familiar puppy was in the room. Later, when Mom said she was heading to Miss Penny's to pick up the Bean, Charles volunteered to go with her. And when they got back home, Charles offered to play with the Bean, helping him put down tracks on the new train table Dad had set up in the den.

"That would be so helpful." Mom began to put pans on the stove and pull things out of the fridge. "I was hoping to get dinner started."

The Bean had already headed for the den, and

now Charles could hear him yelling. "No, no, no, no, no!" he wailed.

"Oh, dear." Mom rolled her eyes and put down the onion she had just picked up.

"I'll see what it is." Charles bolted for the den. What could be the matter?

He stopped at the door, staring at Molly, who was nudging the Bean up against the train table. "No, Molly!" Charles cried.

Molly turned to stare back at him. The light brown spots over her eyes twitched, making her look bewildered — or maybe, Charles thought — angry.

What did I do? Why are you mad? I was just trying to be friendly.

The Bean had stopped yelling by then, probably out of pure terror. Charles clapped his hands.

"Here, Molly," he said. "Time for you to go out-side." He marched toward the back door, checking over his shoulder to make sure the puppy was fol-lowing him — and moving quickly so that she couldn't quite catch up to him and bite him from behind.

"Out," he said, opening the door that led onto the deck and the fenced backyard. She would be safe out there, and he could keep an eye on her from the window in the den. "Go play." He stood carefully out of the way and watched Molly slip outside.

"Everything okay?" Mom asked.

"I think so," said Charles. He went back to the den and checked the Bean all over, looking care-fully to make sure he had not been bitten. "Did Molly hurt you?" he asked.

The Bean shook his head and jammed his thumb in his mouth.

Charles decided to let it go. He didn't want to scare his little brother. "Let's set up the tracks," he said. "I think we should put a big bridge right here." He went over to the train table and began to move things around. Once in a while he glanced out the window to check on Molly. Every time he looked, she was just sniffing around the yard, checking things out.

The Bean loved his new train table. He jumped up and down happily when Charles put together an engine and three cars and made them go around the new track they'd made. "Whoo, whoo!" they both shouted, as the train rolled past the tiny town with its pretend trees and lake.

Charles glanced up one more time to see what Molly was doing. At first he didn't see her. Then he spotted the glossy brown-and-black pup. She was trotting across the yard, carrying something in her jaws. A drooping, squirming something.

"Molly, no! Drop it," Charles yelled out the window. Then he turned to shout to his mom and Lizzie. "Help! Molly caught something."

CHAPTER FIVE

Charles stood at the window for a moment, watching Molly trot straight across the backyard. She looked just as proud and happy as Buddy always did when he grabbed up one of his toys, shook it, and pranced around the room showing it off. Charles shuddered. This was horrible! Why had he ever thought it would be a good idea to foster a vicious dog?

"Molly's bad," reported the Bean. "Bad puppy."

He was only saying that because he had heard Charles yell. Fortunately, the Bean was too little to see out the window. Charles definitely did not

want his little brother to see Molly with an animal in her mouth.

"Stay here. Don't move. Be good." Charles sat
his little brother on the floor and pointed to a pile
of train cars. "Put a nice long train together for
me, okay?"

Charles dashed to the back door and met Lizzie
and his mom on the deck. All three of them stared
at Molly's retreating rear end as she trotted back
into the farthest corner of the yard, out where a
hammock was strung between two tall pine trees.

"Ew," said Lizzie. "This has never happened
before. Do you think it's a squirrel, or what? What
do we do?"

Mom's mouth was a thin, straight line. "We go
try to get it away from her before she has it for
dinner." She marched out into the yard, follow-
ing Molly.

Charles and Lizzie shrugged at each other, then followed Mom.

"Where did she go?" Mom muttered, pushing through bushes and peeking under low-hanging pine boughs. "It's not like the yard is that big. And the gate is closed; she can't have gotten out."

Once, a puppy had escaped from their yard, by digging under the fence. Charles remembered how terrible it had been when Ziggy, the dachshund they had been fostering, ran off and got lost. But Molly had not had nearly enough time to dig a hole big enough for her stocky body to squeeze through.

"Look." Lizzie pointed to a large bush near the fence. Its branches grew down toward the ground, making a little cavelike area underneath. "Shhh!" She tiptoed toward the bush, slowly and silently, with Mom right behind her.

Charles was not sure he wanted to follow too

closely. What if Molly tried to defend her catch? She might charge out at them with ears laid back and teeth flashing. He hung back, waiting to see what Mom and Lizzie found. They bent over near the bush and peeked into Molly's hideout.

"Oh, my," said Mom, in a hushed voice. "Oh, Molly."

"That is so sweet." Lizzie sighed and put a hand on her heart.

"Sweet?" Charles asked. That made him curious, and he inched closer. "What do you mean?"

"Molly hasn't hurt anything. She's just helping to take care of a newborn kitten." Mom straightened up. She looked back toward the house. "And I think I know who it belongs to." She pointed to the sleek black-and-white cat picking her way toward them, a limp, dangling *something* hanging from her mouth. "Here comes Mama, with another one. She must be moving her litter of newborns to a quieter place. I wonder where she gave birth to them."

Charles watched as the cat made her way through the yard. He had heard before of the way that a mama cat will carry her kittens by the napes of their necks, but he had never seen it in real life. It was amazing how the mother cat could grip the kitten so firmly and so gently at the same time. The kitten hung down in limp trustfulness, not struggling at all.

Now the cat ducked into the bushes. Ignoring the humans completely, she settled the new kitten next to its littermate, who lay snuggled in the curve of Molly's big body. She nuzzled them both, then touched noses with Molly. Molly's stubby tail gave a gentle, reassuring wag.

They'll be safe here, I promise.

The mother cat turned and headed back across the yard, probably to fetch another kitten. Charles scootched down under the bush next to Lizzie, to get a better look. The kittens must have heard him; they turned their faces toward him and he saw that they were so young that their eyes weren't even open yet. One of them was a tiger-stripey gray, and the other was black and white like its mom. Their tiny ears were the size of Charles's pinky nail. The tiger cat yawned, its pink mouth open wide, and stretched out a minuscule paw toward Charles. "Ohhh," he said. He had never seen anything so — so what? He didn't even have words for the way it made his heart feel when he looked at Molly and the kittens.

In an instant, all his fears disappeared. How could he have ever been afraid of this amazing puppy? A dog who would help a mama cat move

her kittens was not a dog who would hurt anyone, ever.

Then Molly looked up. Her ears perked. She
sniffed at the air and cocked her head.

I hear something. Somebody needs me.

She got to her feet — gently so as not to bother
the kittens, but quickly. She headed toward the
house with a purposeful trot. When Charles
turned to watch her go, he heard it, too. The Bean
was crying.

"The Bean," he said. "He's all alone in the den!"

They all ran toward the house. When Charles
pushed the back door open, Molly nosed her way
past him and streaked through the kitchen, a
brown-and-black blur.

By the time they caught up with her, she had
already done her magic. The Bean sat on the

floor, wiping his tearstained cheeks, while Molly stood over him protectively, leaning her solid body against his as if she were a big, heavy blanket. She snuffled at his hair and gently licked his face. "Where were you?" the Bean wailed, when he saw Charles and the others. "I was all by myself!"

"We're here now." Mom swooped down to pick him up and give him a big squeezy hug. "Everything's okay, Beany. We're here now."

Charles went over to pet Molly. "I'm sorry," he whispered into her soft brown ear. "I'll never be scared of you again. I promise." Now he knew that Molly must have been comforting the Bean earlier, too — and instead of praising her, he had thrown her into the backyard. He also knew just where the sleek black-and-brown pup would be sleeping that night: right at the foot of his bed.

CHAPTER SIX

"Chickens!" The Bean pointed and laughed his googly laugh.

Sure enough, Charles saw a whole flock of chickens, milling about behind a low fence. There were red ones and white ones and ones with black and white spots, and all of them were clucking and scraping the ground with their feet and rustling their feathers and doing their chicken thing.

Charles held tightly to Molly's leash. He wasn't sure what she would do when she spotted the chickens. Would she want to chase them? Probably not, but you never knew.

Charles and the Bean and Mom were at Fable Farm on this green and sunny afternoon, checking things out in advance for the field trip from Penny's Place. They had brought Molly along at Lizzie's suggestion. "She needs socialization," Lizzie had said. "It's important to expose a puppy to lots of different environments and people. The farm will be perfect."

The farm *was* perfect. It seemed like a place out of the past to Charles, with its big white farmhouse and faded red barn surrounded by gardens bursting with flowers and herbs and vegetables. In the center of the yard was a huge, old, spreading apple tree with a wooden swing hanging from one big branch. The farm was quiet and peaceful, and the people they had met so far, Jesy and Jonny, were so nice. They both had big smiles and muddy, bare feet. Charles remembered Jesy from the farm stand where his family sometimes bought corn.

Now Molly glanced up at Charles. She gave him that doggy smile of hers, but this time he wasn't afraid of the white teeth he saw. This time, he smiled back — and she seemed to understand that he was happy with her, even without him petting her or saying a word. Her stubby tail wagged and she shook her head so her ears flapped. She yawned and stretched out her front feet.

This is worth leaving my kitty friends for.

"Good girl, Molly." Charles scratched her ears. Over the last couple of days Charles had begun to realize that this was the sweetest, gentlest puppy he had ever met. She was like an aunt to those kittens out in the backyard. She spent time with them every day, watching over them whenever the mother cat was away.

Charles knew that the kittens — and the mother cat — would soon be going to Caring Paws, the animal shelter. He and Lizzie had looked all over the neighborhood for lost-cat signs, and checked with the police and all the local vets, but nobody had reported a missing cat. Now he looked at the big red barn and wondered if the farmers might like a kitten or two. He knew that lots of farmers liked to have cats in their barns, to keep the mice away. He glanced over to the farmhouse back porch, where Mom sat talking with Jesy.

By now, Charles and Molly and the Bean had wandered closer to the chicken pen, and the Bean was calling to the biggest, reddest chicken. "Come here, chickie-chickie-chickie," he sang, poking his fingers through the fence.

"She doesn't like to play." Charles turned to see a little girl with white-blond hair. She looked familiar, and he remembered seeing her with Jesy at the farm stand, one day when he was searching for Ziggy, that lost foster puppy. The girl pointed to the red chicken. "That one's name is Esmerelda and she is scared of people. You have to call Bonita, the white one. Over there."

The Bean stared at the girl. "Who are you?" he asked.

"I'm Meridian," she said. "I live here. I take care of the chickens. And the ducks, too."

The Bean's eyes widened. Charles was surprised, too. Meridian didn't look much older than the Bean. "That sure is a big responsibility," said Charles.

"Mommy helps." Meridian pointed toward Jesy. "But I find all the eggs. And I feed them every morning. Sometimes the chickens even peck me, if they're in a bad mood."

The Bean's eyes widened even more and he moved away from the fence.

Molly pushed her nose into Meridian's hand, looking for some petting. "Oh!" said Meridian. "Is this your dog?"

"We're fostering her," said Charles. "We just have her for a little while until we find her a forever home. Her name's Molly."

"She's nice," said Meridian. "We already have a dog, though. Come on, want to meet the ducks?" She headed off confidently toward a silvery, round pond at the bottom of a long, grassy hill.

Charles looked toward the farmhouse. Now Jesy was showing Mom the flower gardens. He waved to them. "We're going to see the ducks," he called.

"We'll be right behind you," Mom called back.

"Let's go," Charles said to the Bean, and they followed Meridian.

When they caught up to her, Meridian began to chatter about the ducks. "They sleep with the chickens but in daytime they like the pond best," she said. "The white one is named Juliet, the brown one is Rapunzel, and the brown-and-white one is Sandra. The one with green feathers on his neck is a boy. His name is Romeo, and a fox once tried to get him, but he got away. He . . ."

She chattered away, and Charles kept nodding and smiling, but the Bean got bored and ran on ahead. "Don't go too close to the pond," Charles called out.

But the Bean did not seem to hear him. He raced down the hill, through the long green dandelion-spangled grass. Molly began to gallop after him, and Charles had to run to keep up with her.

"Wait up!" Charles yelled.

"Catch him!" Mom shouted, from behind Charles.

The Bean laughed his googly laugh and kept running. Then, all of a sudden, he seemed to trip and fall, and the next thing Charles knew, the Bean was tumbling and rolling right down the bank of the pond. "No!" Charles yelled. Any second now his little brother would splash into the water — and there wasn't a thing he could do about it.

CHAPTER SEVEN

Charles felt the hair on the back of his neck stand up. Even if he ran as fast as he could, he would not be able to catch up to the Bean. How deep was the water in that silvery pond? Maybe it was just a few feet deep, but the Bean was only a few feet tall. Even a shallow pond was too deep for someone who could not swim.

Molly gave one loud bark and charged forward, pulling the leash right out of Charles's hand.

"Mom!" Charles turned to see if his mother was getting closer. She was flying down the hill, but she was still even farther away from the Bean than he was.

He turned back, expecting to see the Bean land in the water with a splash. Instead, he saw Molly — wonderful, amazing Molly! — barreling down the hill like a speedy little locomotive, until the last minute when she leapt like an Olympic high jumper, right over the Bean's rolling body. Then she planted herself, solid as a rock, between him and the water. Smack! The Bean rolled into the black-and-brown pup — and stopped.

"And then the Bean looked up at Molly and laughed. Just laughed and laughed, because he didn't even know that she might have just saved his life," Charles said at morning meeting the next day at school. Charles had bounced up and down waving his hand until Mr. Mason called on him to share. He could hardly wait to tell how Molly had saved the Bean from rolling into the pond. He could see it now, the way she had raced through the grass, her powerful legs driving her strong, sturdy body down the hill. She had run so fast! Faster than Charles would have ever thought she could go. In seconds she had caught up with the Bean.

Charles remembered how the ducks had flapped their wings and squawked, and how Mom had swooped down the hill to grab up the Bean in her arms, and how Jesy had talked on and on about what a hero Molly was.

"Wow," Charles's friend David said now. "Did you tell Molly she was a good girl?"

Charles nodded. "I hugged her and patted her and told her over and over. Man!" He shook his head. "I never saw a dog do something like that before."

Mr. Mason smiled. "That's a wonderful story, Charles. Thanks for sharing it. Molly must be a very special dog." He checked his watch. "We need to move on to some math practice, but we'll have some time after lunch today if you and Nicky are ready to give your report about Rottweilers."

Charles looked at Nicky. "I guess we're *almost* ready," he said.

"You can use the computer at recess time if that will help," said Mr. Mason.

And that was how Charles and Nicky ended up staying inside at recess, downloading pictures of dogs, instead of playing four-square outside on the playground. It was worth it, to have the report done. By the time the rest of their class came back in, they were ready.

Mr. Mason got everyone quieted down and seated at their desks. Then he had Charles and Nicky come to the front of the class. Charles had a folder with their report in it — or at least their notes, plus a bunch of pictures.

Charles had not minded doing the research for the report. He had learned a lot about Rottweilers. But standing up in front of the class and talking was definitely not one of his favorite things to do. He nudged Nicky. "You start," he said. He looked through the folder and pulled out one of the best pictures they'd found, of a happy Rottweiler running toward the camera with a big doggy smile on his face. He held it up.

"Rottweilers," said Nicky. "Some people say they are the most misunderstood dog breed, next to pit bulls. Now that I've learned about them, I think that's true. I was one of the people who thought they were all mean and vicious. Now I know they can be nice. Partly because of doing this report, and partly because of hearing about Molly."

He went on to talk about all the things he and

Charles had learned about Rottweilers. "They originally came from Germany," he said, "and they were used as farm dogs, like for herding cows. They are loyal and protective, and usually very calm. Sometimes they don't trust strangers right away, but once they get to know you they will like you."

By then, Charles had gotten used to standing up in front of the class. He was ready to talk. He explained that because Rottweilers are big and strong and smart, some people like to train them as guard dogs. "That's part of why they got such a bad reputation for being fierce," he said. "But they don't have to be that way. They can be great with children and with other animals. I even found an article about a Rottweiler who spends time at a day-care center every day and helps keep the kids happy and calm. Rottweilers are great dogs, as long as they have strong, confident owners who teach them to be gentle and kind."

When they finished, Mr. Mason led the class in a round of applause. "Excellent job, boys," he said. "I think it's especially interesting that doing this report helped Nicky change his mind about Rottweilers. I think you helped a lot of us change our minds. Next year you will all be learning how to write persuasive letters and essays. Who knows what 'persuasive' means?"

"Like, if you talk somebody into something?" Charles remembered when Lizzie had written a persuasive essay that had helped to find a home for one of their foster puppies. "Help them learn to see something differently?"

"Exactly," said Mr. Mason. "Learning how to write well means that you can share your point of view with other people and convince them to see things your way."

Charles thought about that. If his report had helped convince people in his class about Rottweilers, maybe it could convince somebody else. Maybe, just maybe, he could convince Miss Penny that Molly belonged at Penny's Place after all.

CHAPTER EIGHT

Charles got his chance to talk to Miss Penny sooner than he'd expected. The next afternoon, Mom came to get him after soccer practice and they headed straight to Penny's Place to pick up the Bean. Since they were a little late, all the other kids had already been picked up and they found Miss Penny in the kitchen, cleaning out the sink while the Bean "helped" by pulling all the pots and pans out of one of the cabinets.

Miss Penny smiled when she saw them. "Oh, I'm glad you came at the very end of the day." She pushed back her hair with the back of a wet, soapy hand. "I haven't had a chance to talk to you all week, it's been so busy."

"Molly's doing really well," said Charles right away. He figured that Miss Penny must be wondering about the puppy she had given them to foster.

"So I hear," said Miss Penny. "The Bean talks about Molly all the time. His imagination is really amazing these days. He's made up some incredible tales about her. All the kids love to hear about Molly helping a mother cat move her kittens, or Molly keeping the Bean from falling into the pond. I don't know where he comes up with these wild stories."

"They're not stories!" Charles burst out, before Mom could say a thing. "It's all totally true. That's what I wanted to tell you. Molly really is a hero."

Miss Penny looked surprised. "Really? She did all those things?" She looked at Mom.

Mom nodded. "She did," she said. "I saw it with my own eyes. Molly is a very special dog."

"Special," the Bean echoed. He jumped up and down. "Save me, Molly!"

Charles laughed. "Save you from what?" he asked.

Miss Penny smiled down at the Bean. "It's a new game," she explained. "All the kids have been playing it these last few days, after they heard the stories about Molly. One of them pretends to be in some sort of trouble. Another one pretends to be Molly, and 'saves' them. It's very entertaining."

Charles took a deep breath. "Miss Penny," he said. "I know you didn't think you could take care of a puppy, and I know some people might not think a Rottweiler belongs in a day-care center, but I wish you would give Molly another chance."

Miss Penny wiped her hands on a towel and cocked her head. "Do you?" she asked. "To be honest, I have been feeling a little sad about giving her up. Tell me more."

Charles ran out to the car to grab his report out of his backpack. Then he shared everything he'd learned about Rottweilers with Miss Penny, and showed her pictures, and told her about the website where he'd read about a Rottweiler who spent her days at a day care, helping to take care of the kids.

Miss Penny listened to it all, nodding and smiling. "Well," she said, when he'd finished. "You certainly did a good job on that report, Charles. I must say, you are very convincing. In fact . . . you've persuaded me that Molly might be more of a help than a bother. Now I can see how she might possibly be a part of Penny's Place —"

Charles jumped up. "Yes!" he shouted.

"But —" Miss Penny held up her hand. "But I'm afraid that's not enough. I can't have a dog here unless I have permission from every parent of every one of the children I take care of."

Charles's shoulders drooped. "Oh." That sounded like a problem. What was he supposed to do, go around to everyone's home and give his report, over and over?

"So how about this," Miss Penny said, after thinking for a moment. "What if we invite the parents to an open house meeting about it? You can do your report for everyone, and we can have Molly here for them to meet. I'll talk to my lawyer and write up a permission slip for parents to sign."

"Yes!" Charles shouted again.

"Just remember," Miss Penny said. "Unless every parent agrees, I can't take Molly."

*   *   *

A few days later, after dinner, Charles and his mom took Molly to Penny's Place for the open house. "Remember, be on your best behavior," he told the sleek brown pup, as they walked up to the door. Molly looked up at him with her velvety brown eyes and wagged her stubby tail.

I'm always on my best behavior.

It was funny to see Miss Penny's place full of adults instead of children. Charles smiled to himself when he saw all the grown-ups milling around, imagining them all sitting down to do some finger-painting, or going over to rummage through the dress-up trunk. But they were there for serious business, not for fun. Miss Penny showed everyone to a half circle of child-sized chairs she'd set up, and asked them to sit down. Then she invited Charles up to the front of the group to introduce Molly and give his report.

Charles looked out at all the faces and gulped. This was a lot harder than giving a report to his classmates. But then he glanced down at Molly, who sat perfectly still at his side, and he remembered what it was all about. "This is Molly," he began. "She's a Rottweiler. Rottweilers are one of the most misunderstood breeds in America." After that, the rest of the report went perfectly. Charles added the true stories of all the helpful things he'd seen Molly do. "And if anyone wants a kitten, by the way, the ones in our yard will be available for adoption pretty soon," he finished. "They'll make wonderful cats, because they've had the best nanny in the world."

Afterward, lots of parents came up to meet Molly and shake her paw. Charles saw people stopping on the way out to sign permission slips,

66

too. Just as he was about to head outside to give Molly a chance to do her business, one last parent came up to introduce herself to Charles. "I've heard a lot about this dog," the woman said. "I'm Gail, Daniel's mom. You know, Spidey?" She smiled. "I thought Daniel had made up all those stories about Molly, but I guess not." She eyed Molly nervously. "She's big for a puppy, isn't she?"

Charles nodded. "But she's very gentle. Would you like to shake her paw?"

Gail stepped back. "Maybe another time. I — I'm kind of afraid of dogs, I guess." She looked embarrassed. "I got nipped by a dachshund when I was a little girl, and ever since then I'm just nervous around them." She rubbed her hands together. "I came tonight because I really wanted to be open to your idea. I don't want Daniel and his little brother, Aaron, to grow up afraid of dogs the way I am."

"I understand," said Charles. "Thanks for coming tonight to meet Molly." Charles really did understand about being afraid of dogs, now more than ever. But he felt his stomach sink as he watched Gail leave a few minutes later — without stopping to sign a permission slip.

CHAPTER NINE

Charles thought about it as he got ready for bed that night. He frowned at himself in the mirror as he brushed his teeth, feeling glum. He'd done his best, but it had not been enough. All the parents had signed permission slips — except for Gail. After everyone had left the open house, Miss Penny had tried to cheer him up. "Gail's a wonderful mom," she had said. "She only wants the best for her boys. Give her some time — maybe she'll change her mind one of these days." She looked doubtful, though.

Maybe Charles's great idea was just not going to work out. He felt bad about that. But in a way, he felt even worse for Gail and her boys. After his experience with Molly, he knew only too well that it was no fun being afraid of dogs. After all, the world was full of dogs. They were everywhere you went. Big dogs, little dogs, guard dogs, neighborhood dogs. You really couldn't avoid them completely. What kind of life would it be for Daniel and Aaron if they were not comfortable around dogs? They would miss out on all the wonderful things about dogs. Charles could hardly stand to think about never hugging a dog, or letting one kiss you on the cheek or put a paw on your lap.

When Mom came to tuck him in, Charles sat up in bed and told her what he was thinking. "It's not just about the permission slip," he said. "Even if Gail never signs one, I just want her — and Daniel and Aaron — not to be scared of dogs."

Mom smoothed his hair. "That's a nice thought," she said. "What if I call Gail right now and invite Daniel over for a playdate with the Bean tomorrow? She could bring Aaron, too, and have some coffee with me while the boys play. Maybe just a little more exposure to a gentle dog like Molly would help."

Gail and her boys came over the next day, straight from Miss Penny's. Charles met them at the door — without Molly. The Rottweiler pup and Buddy were both up in his room, with the door closed. Charles wanted to make sure Gail and her family felt comfortable — *before* they met any dogs. He had spent his recess time on the computer again that day, searching for ways to help people overcome a fear of dogs. One of the main things he'd learned was that it was good to take things slowly. Now he opened the door wide to the family on his doorstep. Daniel stood grinning up at him while little Aaron, in Gail's arms, held tight to a blue stuffed rabbit. "Come on in," he said.

"Where's Molly?" Daniel demanded.

"Mowwy, Mowwy, Mowwy!" Aaron chanted, waving his bunny.

Gail smiled and shrugged. "They've heard so much about her," she said. "They really can't wait to meet her in person."

"That's great," said Charles. "But let's just go sit down and talk first." He led them into the living room, where Mom was waiting with the Bean, a plate of cookies, and a mug of coffee for Gail. They all sat down, and Charles told the boys a little bit about how to behave around a real dog. At recess, he'd read that learning to understand some doggy language could help people tell when a dog was friendly. "A happy dog has her tail up and wagging, and her ears are this way" — he made perky ears with his hands — "not this way." He made his hands go back the way a fearful or angry dog's might go. "Her mouth might be open a little bit and you might even see her teeth, but that just means she's smiling."

Daniel and Aaron thought that was very funny. "Dogs can smile?" Daniel asked.

"Of course, silly!" yelled the Bean.

Charles laughed and went on with his lesson, remembering the things he had read that day. "If you don't know a dog, always ask the owner first if you can pet her. If the owner says yes, stand very still and let the dog come to you. The dog will probably sniff you," he said. "That's how they get to know you. She might even lick you."

Daniel and Aaron giggled again. "*Now* can we meet Molly?" Daniel asked, bouncing up and down on the couch. Aaron bounced, too, on his mom's lap.

Charles looked at Gail. She nodded, but she had that nervous look again. As he went upstairs to get Molly, Charles crossed his fingers, hoping his plan would work.

"Here she is," he said, as he came back into the room with Molly on a leash. Daniel, who had climbed to the top of the easy chair his mom was sitting on, jumped down and began to run toward Molly and Charles.

Mom held the Bean tight on her lap, even though he squirmed to get down. "Let Daniel meet Molly first," she said to him.

"Hold on there, Spidey." Charles held up a hand to slow Daniel down. "Remember, you stand still and let her come up and sniff you. Then, if you're ready, you can try petting her. Start with her body, not her head."

74

Gail sat up straight and watchful with Aaron on her lap as Daniel froze like a statue, waiting for Molly to sniff his outstretched hand. Daniel petted the puppy on her side, then threw his arms around her and hugged her tight. Charles saw Gail's eyes widen, but Molly's stubby tail just wagged, and she gently licked Daniel's cheek.

No need to be afraid, little one.

Gail let out a breath, and her face relaxed. Charles couldn't help grinning. It was working. Already, Gail seemed to be more comfortable around Molly.

Aaron started to cry. "Shhh, shhh, what is it?" Gail asked, rocking him in her arms.

Charles felt Molly tug on the leash. The puppy pulled him over toward Gail, then bent her head to the floor, then lifted it again — with Aaron's blue rabbit in her mouth. Gently, Molly pushed it into Aaron's flailing hand. His sobs stopped instantly. He looked at the puppy and smiled.

"What do you say?" Gail prompted him.

"Thank you, doggy." Aaron ducked his head, then peeked out at Molly and grinned. "Mowwy!"

Charles could not believe how well things were going.

Then Aaron started to cry again. Gail patted his bottom. "I think someone needs a fresh diaper." She got to her feet with Aaron in her arms. "Is there a bathroom downstairs?"

Mom was telling her where to go when a shrieking whistle arose from the kitchen. "Oops, I must have left the teakettle on," said Mom. She got up and went out of the room, right after Gail.

"Come see my train table." The Bean tugged on Daniel's arm and the two of them raced out of the living room.

Charles looked at Molly.

Molly looked back at Charles. She opened her mouth in a doggy smile and thumped her tail.

I'm a good girl, aren't I?

"That's right." Charles scratched her between the ears. "You are a good girl. A very good girl."

Then he heard a bang. And a crash. And a yell.

"Save me, Molly!"

CHAPTER TEN

"Save me, Molly, save me!" It was Daniel's voice. Charles felt his stomach twist into a knot. What kind of trouble had Spidey gotten himself into now? But he had no time to wonder. The second Molly heard her name she responded, charging toward the den like a racehorse heading for the finish line.

Charles tore after her.

He skidded to a stop just inside the door of the den, with Mom and Gail close at his heels. "What —" He stared at Daniel and the Bean, who both stood up on top of the train table, grinning as they threw cabooses, engines, and freight cars down onto the floor. Neither of them seemed to be in the least bit of trouble. They were obviously just having fun.

Molly had both paws up on the edge of the train table. Her head was cocked as she stared at the boys, looking bewildered.

I thought you needed help!

"You boys, come on down from there." Mom stepped into the room. "That train table isn't for standing on."

"And you can't call Molly like that, if it's not really an emergency," Charles said. "It's not a game to her. She takes it seriously if she hears someone calling for help. Understand?"

Daniel and the Bean climbed down off the table and stood looking down at their feet. "Sorry," said the Bean, in his tiniest voice.

"Sorry." Daniel kicked at a red caboose near his sneaker.

So far, Gail hadn't said a thing. Now she looked down at Charles. "Do you have one of those permission slips here? I'm ready to sign."

The next afternoon, Charles stood near the little pond at Fable Farm, watching the Bean act out a very dramatic retelling of the way Molly had saved him from splashing into the water. It was the big field trip day, and all the Penny's Place kids were having a blast. They had already found eggs in the chicken shed, chased the geese, picked cherry tomatoes off the twining vines, swung on the swing, and searched for raspberries in the tall, prickly bushes in back of the barn.

Charles looked down at Molly, who sat patiently by his side. He should have been happy. He should have been proud. He should have felt satisfied with a job well done. After all, he had convinced every single parent to sign a permission slip so Molly could be at Miss Penny's.

But there was a problem.

Gail had only signed on one condition: that she and her boys could be the ones to adopt Molly. "It's not a waste to have all those slips signed," she'd said, as her pen raced over the bottom of the form. "Now she can go with the boys when they go to Penny's Place." She'd handed the slip to Charles. "It's perfect."

Not only that, when they had arrived at the farm, Jesy had approached Charles and his mom. "Jonny and I have been talking it over all week," she said. "We've decided that we'd love to give Molly a home here at the farm. She's an amazing dog, and we want her to be part of our family. What do we need to do to adopt her?"

Charles knew that Miss Penny wanted to adopt

Molly, too. She wanted to make Molly a part of Penny's Place.

This had never happened before, in all the time that the Petersons had been fostering puppies. Finding one perfect forever home for each puppy was usually the hard part. Now they had to decide between *three* perfect forever homes.

Charles knew that Molly could be very happy as the day care's mascot. She seemed to enjoy being around kids, and she had a natural drive to take care of people — and animals — who needed her help.

On the other hand, Gail and her two boys could be a perfect family for Molly. Charles was so happy that Gail was overcoming her fear of dogs. He knew that Molly would love being around Daniel and Aaron as they grew up.

Then there was the farm. What a great place for a dog. There was room to roam, a pond to wade in, animals to herd, another dog to play with, and a family waiting with open arms.

Charles groaned. "How are we supposed to decide?" he asked Mom, who had come to stand next to him. He looked up the hill toward the farmhouse and saw Gail, Jesy, and Miss Penny standing near the flower garden, deep in conversation. "Do you think they're fighting about which one of them gets to keep Molly?"

Mom put an arm around his shoulders. "I hope not," she said. "But we'll find out soon. Here they come."

The three women walked down the hill together. They didn't look as if they were fighting. In fact, they looked happy. As they got closer, Molly stood up and began to wag her stubby tail.

They stopped just in front of Charles and stood with smiles on their faces.

Molly pulled on the leash, and Charles let her

go. She went straight to Miss Penny and sat in front of her, smiling up at her with that special doggy smile.

"She knows!" Gail clapped her hands.

"She does?" asked Charles. "What does she know?"

"She knows where she belongs. We've all agreed that Miss Penny's is the best place for Molly. Daniel and Aaron can see her there —"

"— and so can Meridian," said Jesy. "She wants to go to Miss Penny's now, too. And if Miss Penny ever needs to go away on vacation, she'll have at least two families who would love to take care of Molly."

"It just seemed like the right thing to do," said Miss Penny. "It's what my aunt wanted in the first place, after all." She knelt to pet Molly. "You are going to be the perfect addition to Penny's Place," she told the pup. Molly's stubby tail began to wag as she licked Miss Penny's face. Miss Penny smiled up at Charles.

Mom put an arm around Charles's shoulders and bent down to whisper into his ear. "You did it," she said. "I'm proud of you."

"I'm proud of Molly," said Charles. "She's the one who taught us all a lesson, about not judging someone on their looks. All we had to do was pay attention."

PUPPY TIPS

A while ago I read an article online about a dog who helps out at a day-care center. I thought it was such a great idea, and I wanted to base a book on it. In the story I wrote, Molly is accepted for what she is and how she behaves, instead of being judged because of her breed. I wish this could always happen in real life, but unfortunately many people are prejudiced against certain breeds like pit bulls and Rottweilers.

Of course, it's wise to be cautious around any dog you do not know, no matter what breed he is. Always ask the owner before you approach a dog, and remember to move slowly and let the dog sniff you before you pet him.

Dear Reader,

The first dog I had as a grown-up was a Rottweiler mix named Jack who I rescued from an animal shelter. He was a very handsome dog, and mostly very well-behaved. Except for the time when he and another dog, a golden retriever named Molly, ate all the books off my bookshelf when I was away! They tore up the couch, too. I guess they had quite a party. I was pretty mad at the time, but of course I forgave them.

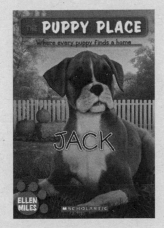

Yours from the Puppy Place,
Ellen Miles

P.S. For a book about another dog who likes to eat things he shouldn't, check out JACK! I named this boxer puppy in honor of my dog.

THE PUPPY PLACE

DON'T MISS THE
NEXT PUPPY PLACE
ADVENTURE!

Here's a peek at LIBERTY!

"When will they start?" Lizzie Peterson leaned into her mother's warm hug. She hated to admit it, but she was so sleepy she could hardly keep her eyes open. Still, there was no way she was going to miss the fireworks. She'd been looking forward to them ever since she'd learned that her family was going to Brisco Beach for the Fourth of July.

Lizzie had been hearing about Brisco Beach for years. Her cousins Stephanie and Becky went there every summer. It was a tiny town, mostly made up of vacation cottages, way out on a long, narrow spit of land between the ocean and the bay. Stephanie loved to talk about Brisco Beach. Lizzie had heard about the bay side (shallow, no waves, great for swimming or paddling in a kayak) and the ocean side (big waves for body-surfing, great for building sandcastles at low tide). She'd heard about the cottages (adorable, and each with its own cute name), the Snack Shack (best fries anywhere!), Captain Stark's fishing pier (a long, rickety boardwalk that extended far into the ocean, held up by tall wooden pilings), and The Point (groovy surf shop, best place to buy a bathing suit or ankle bracelet). Stephanie had told Lizzie how you could ride a bike to any of those places, or walk on the beach for miles, collecting seashells, or, on a rainy afternoon, just lie on the screened-in porch at the cottage and read.

Lizzie thought it sounded like heaven — even without the fireworks. But the fireworks, according to Stephanie, were the very best part. "They don't start until it's dark," she'd told Lizzie that afternoon. "Everybody goes over to the ocean side to wait for them, and there are bonfires all up and down the beach. People play guitars and sing, or have clambakes. We always have hot dogs for dinner and s'mores for dessert. You eat until you can't eat any more, and then the sun goes down and you know the fireworks will happen soon. It gets darker and darker and you wait and wait and wait. It always seems like forever. And then — *BOOM!* — the first one goes off."

ABOUT THE AUTHOR

Ellen Miles loves dogs, which is why she has a great time writing the Puppy Place books. And guess what? She loves cats, too! (In fact, her very first pet was a beautiful tortoiseshell cat named Jenny.) That's why she came up with the Kitty Corner series. Ellen lives in Vermont and loves to be outdoors every day, walking, biking, skiing, or swimming, depending on the season. She also loves to read, cook, explore her beautiful state, play with dogs, and hang out with friends and family.

Visit Ellen at www.ellenmiles.net.